BERBER

A Lamb's Tale

Margaret Anderson Johnson

BERBER
A Lamb's Tale

By Margaret Anderson Johnson

Published By:
WaterOak Publishing
6056 Thomasville Road
Tallahassee, FL 32312

Library of Congress Catalog Card Number : 99-94017

ISBN: 0-9663170-0-9

Printed by: Times Publishing Group, Malaysia.
10 9 8 7 6 5 4 3 2 1

Cover art and all illustrations by Margaret Anderson Johnson

Author photo courtesy of Lynn Ivory, Master Photographer, Tallahassee, Florida

Dedication

To all who loved little Berber Lamb and appreciated his special qualities and all who didn't know Berber but understand the importance of proclaiming, to precious human lambs, the unique Lamb of God.

ౚ   ౚ   ౚ

We thank God for the joy, pleasure and devotion of this special living creature for a season.

Acknowledgments

The story of Berber has many authors. Still, it is his story and only he could tell it.

Heartfelt gratitude to:

My Tommy, who proofread, over and over again...always through tears.

To Wendy for ruthless editing, generous appreciation and laughter.

To Laura for innumerable proofreadings, her way with words... and more.

To Rebecca, T.J. and Susan for their fresh, modern approach.

To Beth and Bubba for naming Berber and for listening so many times to his story.

To Jack for quality counsel, but most of all for identifying Berber's conflict as only an expert shepherd could.

To Alan and Carolyn for professional expertise.

To Beth and Al, Virginia, Marnie and Makay for advice, ideas, etc. and to C.J....what can I say?

To the "cutest little creatures I ever laid my eyes on": Anna, Beth, C.J., Danny, David, Dougie, Kiara, Michael, Nicole, Samuel, Steven, Tierra and Quinton for being there and for loving Berber.

Special thanks for the interest and moral support of *many* other dear friends.

...and to Mark, he knows why!

Berber was a little lamb,

His wool was sparkling white,

He always stood up straight and tall,

And was a handsome sight.

CHAPTER ONE

My name is Berber. I am a lamb. I didn't always *know* I was a lamb. In fact, I was quite shocked to discover I wasn't really human. I just thought I was a little different because I walked on four legs and my Mother walked on two.

But, before I get ahead of myself, let me tell you how it all began…

I entered the world on a freezing, windy, night and almost didn't make it because I was abandoned and lost in the terrible storm. Weak and alone, I had given up all hope of ever being saved, but a good shepherd found me before it was too late. It seemed God had a plan for my life.

The good shepherd wrapped me in warm blankets and sheltered me from the cold.

That night my mother came to me.

Although my first memories are pretty hazy, I faintly remember being gently lifted and hearing a voice say, "He's weak and completely helpless. Go quickly. See if you can save him!"

I heard soothing sounds as I felt myself being carried away. Of course, I didn't fully understand what was happening, but I snuggled in the warmth that comforted me. I felt safe and secure.

I woke up the next morning in a cozy place flooded with golden light and full of many wonderful smells. I was busy studying all the interesting things surrounding me, when suddenly, I saw my Mother for the first time!

She was much taller than me and she walked on only two legs. Higher up, she had two more legs she used to hug me and carry me around. But as I looked even higher, I saw the most amazing thing of all: the top of her head was completely covered with soft white wool *just like mine.*

In other ways my Mother looked different from me, but those things were not important. I knew she was my Mom and I knew I was exactly where I belonged.

Maama started feeding me milk from a little bottle right away, and she let me have more milk anytime I wanted it. The milk was warm and it soothed my throat and tummy. Mom held me softly while I drank and I was content.

Most of the time Maama spoke to me in a calm, gentle voice. But every now and then, she made *baaaing* sounds to match what I said when I was trying to tell her how good I felt. Her *baaaing* sounds made me feel close to her.

In the beginning, I didn't understand exactly what Maama was saying, but I always understood she loved me.

I understood, also, that God saved me from the storm that night and gave me my Mom. I was feeling very grateful for God's love and care when I realized I was smiling.

I like to smile.

CHAPTER TWO

During my earliest days I spent most of the time eating and sleeping. In no time at all, I stopped drinking from the little bottle, but I still depended on Mom for my food. I could always tell from the sound she made that it was time to eat and she would guide me to my food bowl. She took care of all my needs and protected me in every way.

When I was thirsty, Mom would lead me to the still waters of a big, big pool. She taught me to kneel and brace myself against the side so I wouldn't fall in while I was drinking. She showed me how to drink slowly so I wouldn't get water up my nose and choke.

After I grew a little, I began munching bushes and grass from the pasture. Mom showed me rich green foliage that was good to eat. Otherwise, I might've nibbled poisonous weeds and gotten sick.

Often, Maama sat beside me and scratched the wool on my back and my head. Oh, how I loved that! I would press my head and body against her and beg for more. As far as I was concerned nothing was more important than making me feel wonderful, and Mom seemed to sense that.

Mom introduced me to some other members of our flock. (I'll tell you more about them later.) We all played together, so I usually had plenty of company. But when my playmates weren't around, and Mom was busy doing things that didn't include me, I had to go about my normal routine of straying and grazing and waiting for Mom to return. I didn't mind, though. I always knew she would come again.

I noticed some of my friends licked themselves, rolled in the grass or scraped up against trees to get dirt off, but I didn't care if I got filthy. I'd just let the dirt stay there and wait for Mom to come and clean it off for me. Very early in life I said to myself, "Just face the facts, Berber, you can't do anything for yourself."

One of my favorite memories from those early days was the method Mom used to keep me clean. Every day or two she would bathe me very gently, with something blue, called "soap." I saw her use the same thing on her own wool. The soap made me sparkling white. After every baaath, Mom kept me warm and cozy and snuggled with me until I was completely dry. Ohh, did that feel goood!

Then, someone had to go and ruin my wonderful baaath time. Whoever it was told Mom that washing me was removing something called "lanolin" from my skin.

You see, lanolin kept the bugs from biting me and protected me from the rain and the cold. However, back then, I didn't understand a thing like that, I just knew I was terribly disappointed. I thought Maama was doing a pretty good job of protecting me, and I loved my baaath times. Mom stopped bathing me though (for my own good, of course), and I missed how good it felt and the attention Mom gave me. Who wants lanolin anyway?

It was easy for anyone to see how much I depended on Maama. She knew all my needs had to be met before I would buckle my front legs and lie down to rest. She provided for my comfort and pleasure before I was aware of needing anything and that kept me content.

When I was truly satisfied, I wanted to settle down on a gently sloping hill, silently look out over my world and thoroughly enjoy chewing my cud.

I must tell you, if you've never had the pleasure of chewing your cud, there is no way to describe how wonderfully fulfilling it is. You'll have to try it sometime (or take my word for it, I guess). I always wanted Mom to come over and join me when I was resting like that, and I couldn't understand why she never did. Do you suppose she was just too busy to stop and chew her cud?

Once, while I was resting and chewing, Maama pointed to me and exclaimed, "Look at my Berber. He is one happy little lamb!"

I had no idea what a lamb was when I heard her say that. "What does she mean?" I thought. "What *is* a lamb? Why *does* she keep calling me that?" Though it didn't seem important at the time, it turned out to be a very significant question.

She was absolutely right about my being happy, though. She first loved me, then I loved her in return. That was the main reason for my constant smile.

I like to smile.

CHAPTER THREE

It didn't take long for me to suspect I was pretty special.

When I was only four days old, Maaama took me on an exciting adventure. We left our familiar surroundings and went to a large, spread-out building.

Once we were inside the building, Maama carried me into a big room. She carefully placed me inside a circle of the cutest little creatures I ever laid my eyes on. They all walked around on two legs like Mom, but they were much smaller, were all different colors and none of them had any white wool on top of their heads. I sensed they were very young, and I should show them how straight and tall I could stand. I stood proudly, and as still as I could, wondering what would happen next.

Then, I began turning around slowly within the circle of young ones so I could study each of them. They were smiling at me and all their eyes were filled with wonder. I thought to myself, "They think I'm special." I remember noticing how content they were, for they sat with their legs folded under them like I did when I was completely satisfied. They reached out to touch me and feel my wool. That was fine with me. Their gentle pats felt good and I always loved attention.

"I turned around slowly within the circle of young ones
so I could study each of them."

That was the first time I ever heard my Maama's name. The young ones were singing, "Margaret had a little lamb, his fleece was white as snow." I understood that Margaret was my Mom, and "fleece" had to refer to our wool, but I still had no idea what a lamb was.

We hadn't been in that big room very long before someone big, and tall, with a deep voice entered the room. Mom said, "Berber, this is Coach." All the little ones yelled out loud, "Hey Coach, look at Berber!"

As I stood in the middle of the room with all my cute, new friends, other creatures started peeping through the door. Being the center of attention like that made me sort of nervous. But with little hands patting me and Mom close by watching over me, I decided to stand as still as I could, though my legs were new and shaky (a most irritating nuisance when one wants to make a good impression).

My instinct told me this would be an ideal time to try out my voice. I lifted my head, drew in as much air as I could and slowly released the most friendly, happy, melodious *baaaaaa* I could manage. Everyone began making noises with their hands and they "oooed" and "aaahed" with their voices.

Coach threw up his hands, shook his head in disbelief, and said, "Oh, Man!" I think Coach appreciated more than any one else what an effort that was for me. I heard him say, "Listen to him, he's only four days old and has a voice like Sinatra." I didn't know what a *Sinatra* was, but I *knew* Coach meant he liked me and thought I had a lovely voice.

You can see why Coach became one of my favorite friends. He enjoyed being around all of God's creatures and took pleasure in helping them learn how to do things. I smiled just thinking about him.

I like to smile.

CHAPTER FOUR

There were many creatures in my life who walked on two legs, and I was closer to some than others. Mom's "Tommy" was unique. He lived in the house with Mom and me. Tommy was quiet and didn't hold me as often as Mom did, but I could tell he was proud of me. It was he, more than Maama, who staged my spectacular personal appearances.

I totally relied on Tommy's staging. As far as I was concerned, his greatest talent was directing me to entertain others and his superb sense of timing was almost a match for mine! He enjoyed breaking up meetings and parties by having me suddenly walk into the room and greet everyone with a quick, friendly, melodious, *baaaa*. People went crazy when we did that!

"Tommy was proud of me."

Tommy would holler out in his strong voice, "Hey, Berber, how 'bout doing your runnin' and kickin' routine?" or, "Have you forgotten how to butt?" His reminders gave me the perfect excuse for performing the particular feats he mentioned. But Tommy never had to remind me to smile!

CHAPTER FIVE

One morning, as mom was carrying me around the house, I began feeling adventurous and decided to explore a little. I surprised Maama by leaping from her arms. Before she knew what was going on, I was out of her sight. I wanted to look around on my own, so I was careful not to *baaa* as I pranced from room to room.

Mom didn't like what I was doing one bit. Her voice got high and squeaky as she ran around calling, "Berber, Berber, where are you?" That was the first time I ever witnessed a "tizzy!"

A *tizzy* is when one acts highly excited, becomes confused and runs around in circles, accomplishing nothing. I was to become very familiar with tizzies. They occurred rather frequently around Mom's house.

Maama couldn't find me because she wasn't able to think — being in her tizzy. I'm ashamed to say, I took advantage of her confusion, because I was curious about some things I had seen in our house. So, I began running and leaping from room to room as fast as I could and even though I heard Mom calling me, I didn't answer. I had important business to attend to.

Next to our sleeping room, I had seen a bright, shiny place. I went straight for it. In that room was a long white object that was open and empty and a smaller one with a lid on it. Suddenly, I noticed — right there in that shiny room with me — a strange looking creature staring at me. I had never seen anyone with white wool all over his body before, but that's what this little guy had. I stopped in my tracks and stared. Being the friendly fellow I was, I wanted to get to know him. I thought we could be friends. But, no matter how hard I tried, I couldn't get close to him. An unseen barrier kept pushing me back, rather rudely, I might add.

The woolly creature was most impolite. He copied everything I did. When the invisible barrier forced me backwards, he smiled a sinister smile and backed up, too. He made fun of me in a cruel, teasing way. If I leapt into the air, he jumped up, too. If I kicked up my heels, he did the same thing. When I stretched my neck to its full capacity, that mean fellow pulled up his neck, as well. And he kept grinning at me the whole time. That was more than I could bear!

I backed off across the room, lowered my head into a butting position and ran straight toward his woolly head. But he charged back and butted me so hard I was flattened on the carpet with my legs sprawled out in four different directions. I could see a big greasy spot on the barrier between us and a large bump was taking shape on top of my head.

I was glad to see the creature was flattened out just like me. At least, I got him, too!

I was still dizzy when Mom finally found me and I greeted her with a rather glazed expression. She said, "Well, there you are, I see you have met your match in that *mirror*." She was sort of laughing when she gathered me into her arms. And I was still smiling.

I like to smile.

CHAPTER SIX

As I grew stronger and a little bigger, Mom prepared a place for me outside our house and encouraged me to stay there more and more often. Being outside so much gave me a chance to become better acquainted with my flock.

Now, I need to tell you my flock was not the usual group you might see grazing in a peaceful, green pasture. None of us looked alike. Some of us walked upright on two legs. Others walked on four legs and the "Wheelers" had round fat rubbery legs on which they rolled. Of course the two legged ones were humans and I called the four legged ones, "Barkers." Even though we were different in many ways, we all roamed around together and got along just fine. Most mornings Maama would take me on walks, and quite often we would be joined by a whole passel of Barkers and humans of various shapes and sizes.

The smallest member of my flock was Tuffi. She was a "bitsy-teeny-weeny" Barker who slept with Mom and Tommy — right in the middle of their bed! Tuffi and I were good friends. When I was a baby, she and I were the same size. But, I grew up, and she didn't. Then, I was so big and she was so tiny she had a hard time keeping up with me. She was forced to take one hundred and twenty-nine steps to each one of mine.

"But...I grew up!"

"My flock."

Tuffi

Tuffi never mentioned this to me, but I had the queerest feeling she, too, had a *fight* with that woolly creature in the shiny room. Her face was all squashed in and I couldn't see her nose at all. I couldn't figure out how she breathed. I didn't want to hurt her feelings though, so I never asked her about it. Someone once said, "She looks like Fu Manchu." Since I'd never seen that particular Barker, I wasn't able to vouch for it one way or the other.

I would have to say my closest buddy was an agreeable Barker named Fewbrick. Fewbrick had a real problem. It was immediately obvious to even the most casual observer that he was afflicted with a severe Tizzy he could not get rid of. The first time I ever laid my eyes on Fewbrick, his opening remark was, "Have you seen any of my bricks?" Of course I hadn't and told him so. I didn't even know what bricks were. As he continued running frantically on his way, he hollered back to me, " I'm a few bricks short of a full load, and I need to find my missing bricks." He added as he circled the house for the third time, "I'm searching for them everywhere." I think someone was playing a dirty trick on Fewbrick. What do you think?

Fewbrick

Often, when I was roaming around with my flock, I enjoyed deliberately falling behind a long distance...then I'd run up as fast as I could and butt the back of whomever I chose to honor with my wonderful surprise. Most of the barkers took immediate offense at this game, but in spite of his peculiar affliction, my friend, Fewbrick enjoyed it as much as I did. The two of us had a grand time playing together.

I told him, "Fewbrick, you can stop your frantic searchin'. As far as I'm concerned, you have all the bricks you need."

I learned quickly that the human members of my flock were as offended by the butting game as the Barkers. They made that quite clear by hollering and screaming when they caught me running at them from the rear. Their voices got high and squeaky. Obviously, tizzies were building up so I left them alone. It really was not necessary for them to be so vocal. I would've stopped with much less protest on their part.

"Berber, get away from that poison ivy!"

When we were on our morning walks, Mom wanted me to stay on the well-worn path she traveled. If I strayed, she would pick up a long stick and prod and push me back to the *right* way. She was so quick, I only got to nibble a few morsels of what I believed to be unusually succulent pasture tidbits.

The first time I strayed, I heard someone in our flock holler, "Get Berber away from that stuff. It's poison ivy." Something grabbed me firmly around the neck and pulled me back to the fold.

Maama said, laughingly, "My rod and my staff are a comfort to that little fellow, whether he realizes it or not!"

Of course, Mom thought she was protecting me when she got me away from that Poison ivy. But, I didn't care what its name was—it was delicious stuff. Sometimes my nose tickled after I ate it. My stomach tickled so much it almost made my smile burst into laughter.

I like to smile!

CHAPTER SEVEN

As time went by, I began to understand Maaama better and started listening more carefully to what she had to say. As I grew older, I began entertaining myself by listening to other humans, and I learned a lot that way.

My ears always perked up when I heard my own name mentioned. That's how I found out about where I came from. It seems I was born on a neighboring sheep farm. Mom described beautiful land with soft, green hills gently sloping downward to join fresh, sparkling water, and a narrow, clay road winding up toward a barn in the other direction. It sounded very nice, but I knew where my real home was.

The farm belonged to a fellow named Jack Conrad. He was the kind and gentle shepherd who handed me to Mom that first night.

Mr. Jack told Mom the night I was born was the coldest night of the year. He told her he went out into the storm to check on his flock and found me alone, cold and unconscious. He took me into his warm barn to revive me, and that's when Mom took me home.

Listening to them talk about how I was protected from the very beginning made me wonder if the Creator didn't want me to stick around for a while, so I could touch the lives of all the creatures I got to know.

⌘ ⌘ ⌘

"Golf Cart" slowly bumped along the road..."

Some time after Mom quit feeding me from a bottle and made a place for me outside, she tried to take me back to Mr. Jack's farm and make it my permanent home. I heard her say she thought I was lonely!

I wasn't the faintest bit lonely! I was beginning to understand a lot of things my flock did and was enjoying all our activities. I felt no need whatsoever for any change.

I tried to tell Mom I did *not* want to go live on the farm, but she didn't pay any attention to my Baaaing objections. She picked me up and placed me next to her in the Wheeler called "Golf Cart." "Golf Cart" slowly bumped along the road as we headed *straight* for the sheep farm. I kept baaaing and nudging Mom all the way in protest, but I guess she thought she was doing the best thing for me.

Mr. Jack greeted us and told Maama to take me on over to the flock. He opened a gate and took me from Maama's arms. Mr. Jack put me down gently on the other side of the gate, closed the gate firmly and left me there! I couldn't believe it! I was quite upset and let out with some pitiful baaaaing. I ran around in circles within the fence where Mr. Jack placed me.

I wanted to frown or scowl but, no matter how hard I tried, I couldn't hold back my natural smile. I *was* able to work up a sorrowful, pleading look in my eyes and I could tell that bothered Maama. But she stuck to her plan. She and Golf Cart drove away and I felt all alone, again.

"Mr. Jack took me from Maama's arms."

There were a lot of four-legged creatures at the farm. All of them were covered with a kind of dirty white wool — not clean and shiny like Mom's and mine and there were no smiles on any of their faces. Most of them were a lot bigger than me, and they weren't friendly at all. In fact, they ganged up on me and butted me and teased me and said, "What do you think you're doing here?" "You're too white and you smell funny." "Who's your Maama, anyway?" One particularly sour old gal sidled up to me and said, "Why don't you just go on back where you belong?" I knew then what true loneliness was! I wanted to be back with my Mom and all the creatures who thought I was so special.

As I wandered by myself along the edges of the fence, I made a wonderful discovery! The fence had a hole in it. I waited until I was sure no one was paying any attention, then I scooted down and scooched through the hole in the fence.

"I found my way home."

From there, it was easy to find my way home, and ohhhh, it was good to be back where I belonged!

But, when Maama saw that I had come home, she had one of her tizzies and took me right back to the farm. I kept on returning home, though. Nothing, not even Mom's tizzies, could stop me. Every time Maama took me to the farm, I waited a few days, then, I would sneak out, follow the winding, clay road, turn in by Mom's barn and go right back to my own fold again. I would stroll along casually, eating and nibbling all along the way, because I felt sure I was in complete control of the situation.

One time I made this journey late at night. It was pitch-black dark. There wasn't even a moon to light my way! That didn't bother me until I heard the humans talking. They said I was very lucky that I hadn't run into any wild animals.

A wild animal really could have hurt me! I couldn't defend myself. I didn't have enough teeth to bite. I didn't have any claws. I couldn't hide in the bushes because my sparkling, white wool attracted attention. I couldn't even run very fast. I counted on Maama to protect me from my enemies.

After I heard about the wild animals, I made my journey during the daytime. I was careful to *baaaa* a lot as I strolled along just to stir up some familiar friends as quickly as possible. The infinite resources of my brain had come through for me. I may have been dependent, but I was not dumb!

This routine went on for quite a while. Mom would take me to the farm, then I would come home—Mom would take me *back* to the farm and I would squeeze through the hole in the fence and return home again. Finally, one day, I heard Maama's Tommy say, "Any old goat who wants to live here that badly ought to be able to stay." Mom agreed with Tommy and I never left home again. My smile got a little bit bigger and a little bit wider, besides…

I like to smile.

"Something new developed between Mom and me."

CHAPTER EIGHT

One day, something new developed between Mom and me. She became my shepherd in addition to being my Mom, and she led me in the right direction all the rest of my life. I had no need for anything else.

For quite a while, without understanding why, I had been longing for a shepherd. I didn't know it was simply the natural instinct of a lamb! At that time, I didn't even know I *was* a lamb. But let me tell you how it came about.

I was by myself that particular afternoon because the rest of my flock were wandering off searching for greener pastures. I was minding my own business grazing in my own pasture and drinking from the still waters of the big pool, being careful to brace myself against the edge just as Maama taught me. Suddenly, I heard a voice calling from the back of Maama's house, "Berber, where in the world are you?" I recognized my Mom's voice, but I didn't bother to run to her. I was busy.

However, I absent-mindedly *baaaad* and I heard her say, "Well, come on up here."

Thinking it was possible that Mom had a strawberry to give me, I decided to follow her voice and let her know I was coming to meet her by *baaaing* as I ran in her direction. We kept speaking back and forth to each other until we met somewhere in the middle of the path.

Maama got so excited when she saw me that it made me want to do it again. After that, I almost always did the same thing. Boy, did Mom love it! When she called, "Berber, where are you?" I would answer with a loving, "*Baaaa.*" Then she would reply, "Well, come on up here." You can bet I would run to her as fast as my stubby little legs could carry me, baaaing all the way. Mom would hug my neck and scratch my back and feed me yogurt drops, sometimes M&M's and, best of all, *straaaaaw*berries!

My tail wagged the entire time I was nibbling. Next to my smile and my melodious, *Baaa*, Mom enjoyed seeing me wag my tail.

From then on, I knew Maama was my Shepherd. I knew her voice and I followed her. I suppose all Moms are shepherds somehow. I liked it that way.

I was always obedient—well almost always. I admit there was one time when I deliberately ignored Maama's call. I just couldn't help teasing her a little. It was such fun.

I heard her calling, "Berber, where are you?" Then, I hid behind a large, sprawling, oak tree and watched her searching for me. Her voice got high and squeaky and she ran around in her tizzy again.

When Mom found me she reacted in a funny way. Ordinarily, she called me by my family name, "Johnson." She would say, "Hello there, Berber Johnson. How are you this morning?" I'd *Baaa* for her and she would know from the pleasure in my *Baaa* that I was fine, as usual.

"I heard her calling, 'Berber, where are you'?"

"I hid behind a sprawling oak tree and watched her searching for me."

But this time, when I jumped from behind the oak tree and surprised her, she cried out, "Berber *Conrad*, where in the world have you been?" I had the distinct feeling she was telling me that when I was bad, I belonged next door on Jack Conrad's farm. I knew I had gone too far. But if you had seen the funny look on her face when she was running around in her tizzy, you would have understood why I enjoyed teasing her so much.

That was the only time Maama seemed bothered by the smile on my face. She told me to wipe it off, *right now*. Of course, I couldn't!

I heard her tell her Tommy, "I know he doesn't have a single, mean bone in his sweet, little Berber body, but I swear I think he deliberately pesters me sometimes." She was right.

I may have been smiling on the outside, but I was laughing on the inside!

I like to smile.

CHAPTER NINE

I told you earlier how well the members of my flock got along with each other, and certainly, most of the time we did. But I must tell you about one incident when something, not very nice, happened.

One of the Barkers in our flock was named Crockett. It was his job to take care of Maama. But something must have been bothering Crockett one night, because here's what he did.

While I was having dinner, *in my own pen*, mind you, Crockett started circling the fence and growling at me. I had never heard a growl before. Certainly, I never growled, and I'd never heard Mom do it, either! I had no idea what it meant. So, I just kept on eating, with my ear very close to the side of my pen. Suddenly, Crockett took a *snap* and bit off the top of my ear! I was stunned. No one had ever hurt me before!

"Crockett circled my pen."

I couldn't tend to my own wounds—Maama had to do that for me. A piece of my ear was gone and there was blood flowing all over my snowy, white wool. I hardly knew how to react to this unfriendly behavior. I just stood there in shock. When Mom saw me, she got herself into a shock right along with me. I think she was hanging on the edge of her tizzy.

Maama cried, took me out of my pen and held me close, in spite of the blood all over me. She cleaned me and rubbed some oil on my ear so it would heal. It really didn't hurt all that much, but Mom scolded Crockett and sent him to the barn away from everyone else.

He never bothered me like that again, and I guess I will never know what made him take a nip at me. Maama laughed and told her Tommy, "Crockett must be a member of that Mike Tyson flock." What do you guess she meant by that? Well, everyone else was smiling and I kept on smiling, too.

I like to smile.

CHAPTER TEN

I told you about Crockett "Tyson" biting my ear, because it had a a lot to do with what happened afterwards.

Mom explained to me that I was to play a part in a special drama at a church! She said "Berber, you will make a wonderful Passover Lamb." I didn't know what that was, but if Maama thought it was a good thing, I felt sure I would like it, too.

The day the drama was to be presented, I was placed in a room with a lot of excited humans. They were getting dressed in special clothing they called "costumes." Everyone in the play had a costume, *except for me.*

There was no costume for me!

Someone in the crowd pointed to me and said, "*He* doesn't need a costume," and they all burst out laughing! "What is so funny?" I asked myself. "Why don't I need a costume?" I couldn't believe it! The people around me were putting on fancy clothes and I wanted some, too. I began running around trying to get my point across by butting my head against things and baaaing loudly. Except for dodging my attempts to butt them, though, no one paid one bit of attention to what I was trying to say.

When everyone finished dressing, a man in the most beautiful costume of all picked me up. He was dressed as a priest. He carried me through big double doors into a large room which I recognized immediately as a perfect setting for one of my spectacular personal appearances. But I didn't have a costume!

The church was packed full of people and somewhere I heard *Maaama's* voice. I knew she was not going to like it one bit that I was the only one without a costume. I released a very gentle *Baa* hoping she would help me. I wasn't speaking to anyone else. Nevertheless, everyone loved my *Baaaa*! I heard the crowd exclaim, "Ohhhh!" with unmistakable appreciation as the last strains of my soft *baaa* faded away.

I was already thinking of Baaaing louder to get Maaa's attention when I heard the "Priest" say, "I wouldn't mind if he did that again, right into this mike." That made up my mind. So, I stretched my neck, thrust my head forward right into the face of the thing named "Mike," and sucked in all the air my lungs could hold.

I looked out over all the humans in front of me and saw many eyes looking straight at me. I was searching for Mom's eyes. I opened my mouth and began *baaaaaing*. As I did this, I slowly turned my head from one side of the room to the other. "Mike" followed right along with me! My baaa was so loud it bounced back from "Mike" and blasted out over the entire room.

Every eye stayed on me. I even forgot all about getting Maaama's attention, because I had everyone thrilled over my very loud baaaaa. As was my habit, I enjoyed pleasing a crowd. I had been doing it all my short life. I caught Maaama's expression out of the corner of my eye. I could tell she was proud of me!

"I opened my mouth and began *baaaaaing.*"

In spite of the fact that I was the only one without a costume, I managed to be the hit of the whole show. I had a natural, inborn, ability to become the center of attention, even when operating at a distinct disadvantage.

What happened next turned out to be the most confusing but at the same time the most enlightening moment of my life.

After all the attention I received because of my grandious baaaing, I just settled back quietly in the Priest's arms and listened. The Priest began speaking in a strong, deep voice. He was talking about the sacrifice of the Passover Lamb. (There was that word "Lamb" again, so I listened carefully). He continued speaking about how people in the Bible, in Old Testament times, sacrificed little lambs to show they believed God would send His Lamb to die for the sins of the whole world. The "priest" was looking at me when he talked about the sacrificial lamb

Suddenly, I noticed the Priest was picking up a knife. He was still talking about the Lamb who had to die. Did *I* have to die? Was this Priest going to kill me with his knife? *Was I a lamb?*

A lamb was the last thing I wanted to be if this was the way lambs were treated. If I hadn't been frozen with fear, I would have run out of there as fast as my stubby little legs could carry me.

Since I was being held tightly, I settled down and began tying some things together. I remembered the young humans singing about Margaret's little lamb. I recalled being taken to the sheep farm. And there was no costume for me when I was playing the part of a lamb. Oh, no! I was coming to the miserable realization that a lamb was exactly what I was and they were going to kill me. What could I do? I depended on Maama for everything and she was just sitting there. She didn't even seem worried.

Where was Mom's tizzy when I needed it?

Then, I heard the speaker saying the Passover Lamb had to be perfect. He couldn't have anything wrong with him.

What a relief that was to me! I couldn't fulfill the part of the Passover Lamb, because I had the most wonderful flaw! Do you remember what it was? Right! The top of my ear was missing where Crockett "Tyson" had bitten it off. Thank you, thank you, thank you, Crockett Tyson. You saved my life!

From that day on (though it still bothered me a bit), I knew I was a lamb.

Later, Maama explained to me, "That was only a play, Berber. That's when humans pretend to be someone else to act out a story. They were acting out what people used to do in Bible times. They really wouldn't have done anything to my Berber." I also heard her tell her friends the only way they could've hurt me was, *over her dead body*.

Because of the infinite resources in my brain, I understood about the Passover Lamb, and how wonderful it is that God loved the world so much He sent His own precious Lamb to die in everyone's place. It seems to me that must be the greatest love anyone ever had. I'm smiling, as I think about God's great love.

I like to smile.

CHAPTER ELEVEN

everal months passed by and I had grown quite large by the time the next thing happened. I wanted to tell you about it because it explains why I loved rainy days so much. It also shows how clever I could be.

One afternoon I was wandering around the edge of the big pool. Humans were splashing and playing in its cool, blue waters and I was nibbling on some delicious grass, just relaxing, when something plopped on the end of my nose. It was a rather large spot of water. I looked around. No one was splashing me from the refreshing pool. In fact, no one was anywhere near. I went back to my nibbling — thinking perhaps I was imagining things.

It happened again. Another large drop plopped on my wool top-knot and trickled down the side of my face. I looked up and saw big, dark, fluffy things, stacked high on top of each other, covering the whole sky and making it almost dark in the middle of the afternoon. My heart sank! It made me think of my first night . . .that terrible night when I was lost and alone without any hope.

To make things even worse every single person in the big refreshing pool began to have a tizzy. They ran around in circles, grabbing soft white towels to wrap around their bodies and they all scampered into the house as quickly as they could. I was alone, again, just like that other night!! I was really frightened.

All of a sudden, the dark fluffy things spilled what seemed to be buckets of water all over me. My wool became soggy. I was soaking wet. Since that first night the only time I had been that wet was when Maama was bathing me. But when she bathed me, she always held me close and kept me warm and rubbed me very gently until I was completely dry. What in the world was this? I wasn't even dirty. I needed my Maama.

I leapt up into the air, bucked a few times and performed a couple of sideways kicks just in case someone in the house would notice I was in a state of alarm. But no one came to my rescue.

I ran to the house. Maama wasn't anywhere that I could see. Now that I knew I was a lamb, I needed to learn how to call my shepherd. I began baaing as I had never *baaaad* before and they were not my usual, melodious *baaaas*, they became squeaky bleats in my panic.

You might say I was starting a tizzy of my own. I tried to stop tizzying so I could think instead. What was the best way to rouse Maama, my shepherd?

Quickly, I ran to the door, leaned over, picked up my hoof and began scratching against the wooden door. I followed this by butting the door with all my weight. It made a deafening, thudding noise, which should've roused everybody.

Once again, my ever-resourceful brain had come through. I heard Maama running to the door. She hadn't left me, She had been there all along. She flung the door open and gathered me inside. She could tell I had a tizzy and, understanding tizzies as she did, she wanted to help me as quickly as possible.

She began to rub me with nice, soft, clean towels and kept on rubbing until I was warm and dry. As I told you, I was quite large by this time, but even so, Maama let me crawl into her lap while she completed the job of picking out rosebush thorns, fluffing my wool, scratching my head and rubbing my back.

We cuddled and hugged for a long time, just as we used to when she bathed me. I nuzzled her neck and she pressed her head against mine. It was as if I were a baby lamb again. I felt restored and refreshed. I was satisfied.

I was content.

**"We cuddled and hugged for a long time,
just as we used to when she bathed me."**

After that, I always knew exactly what to do when it rained. I looked forward to it and got excited whenever dark fluffly clouds covered the sky. I couldn't wait for the raindrops. When the first drop sprinkled on my head, I automatically began to think about the pleasure I was going to experience. All I had to do was scratch on the door, and Maama would gather me inside. We would have a cuddling good time. Sometimes, I thought about "accidently" falling into the still waters of the big pool and getting wet when it wasn't even raining!

I kept on growing bigger and bigger until one day, when Maama was standing with a friend, she looked at me and I saw tears in her eyes. I heard her say, "Yes, I know he needs to go live with the other sheep. He might, someday, when he's ready. But he can stay here as long as he wants. He is my precious lamb." I knew that was true.

After all, being a lamb wasn't so bad when you had a Shepherd-Mom like mine. We smiled together! As you know. . .

I like to smile.

"Yes, I know he needs to go live with the other sheep. He might, someday, when he's ready. But he can stay here as long as he wants. He is my precious lamb."

THE LAST CHAPTER

As it says at the top of the page, this is the last chapter. Often, last chapters are written at the end of a fellow's life and that's the way it is with my story, too. But, I don't want *you* to be sad about it. God was in control. In His divine wisdom and power, He chose the way I entered this world, watched over me while I was here and took me out at just the right time.

Perhaps the fact that you are hearing my story helps fulfill the purpose for which I was sent. I hope so. If my life results in showing even one person the importance of following his shepherd, then my time on earth has had true meaning and purpose. Not many of God's creatures can say that at the end of their lives. But I can.

I knew my shepherd, I followed my shepherd, and I was happy all the days of my life. I wish nothing less for you!

Here is how it all happened…

In roaming around with my four-legged friends, the Barkers, I learned a really fun thing to do. As soon as the Barkers heard one of the Wheelers coming around the corner they would perk up their ears and start running and barking and nipping at their rubbery legs. It looked like so much fun, I just had to try it.

I loved it! But the humans didn't like it one bit! Especially Mom. She scolded me and told me not to do it again. She said, "Berber, you'll get hurt, that's a very dangerous thing to do!"

When Maama was around I tried to contain myself. But it was so much fun running and butting my head on those big, fat, rubbery legs that when I thought no one was looking, I sneaked and did it anyway. I guess when one doesn't obey his shepherd, one has to suffer the consequences. And I did.

I thought the Wheelers were friendly. I didn't know they could kill me if their drivers didn't see me. But on my last day that's exactly what happened.

It happened so fast, I didn't feel anything but a big bump. Of course, it wasn't anybody's fault but mine. I could hear and sense how upset everyone was—especially Mom. As soon as she saw that I had been hit, she ran to me crying, "Oh no, not my Berber!" She tried to do something to help me, but there was nothing anyone could do. Mom knew I was dying and I knew it, too. I wasn't afraid, though. My Shepherd-Mom was right there with me.

I heard Maama cry out, "Oh, my precious Berber." The distress in her voice sent a sharp pang through my heart. The look in her eyes told me all her heart wanted to say.

I didn't want Mom to be upset. I wanted her memories of me to be a rare treasure in her life.

I couldn't stand up straight and tall. I didn't have the breath to *Baaaa* for her. So I mustered up the very last ounce of strength I had and wagged my tail as long and as hard as I could...for the last time. It was my way of telling her, "Goodbye, Mom. Don't worry, everything is all right." I heard Mom say. "Oh, look, Berber's wagging his tail for me."

I knew it was just what she needed.

I wanted Maama to know my time with her had been full and complete. I had lived the most wonderful life any lamb could have —a perfect, happy life, full of fun and frolic, kindness, gentleness, tenderness and love!

I didn't mind being a lamb after all. I was secure in the knowledge that some of the lives I had touched would never be the same. Though I strayed from time to time, I fulfilled my role in God's plan and had been just what He desired me to be.

I knew I would live on as Mom's "precious lamb" ...forever.

❖   ❖   ❖

In all my life, no one ever saw me without a smile.

A smile remains on my face, even now.

I like to smile!

"Margaret's precious little lamb."

BERBER

Berber was a lttle lamb,
His wool was sparkling white,
He always stood up straight and tall
And was a handsome sight!

A li'l lady took him in
When he was one day old.
The days they had together were
As rare as purest gold.

Though he was a baby lamb,
He thought he was a child.
He won his way into our hearts,
With his eternal smile.

His Mom loved him as her own.
She couldn't even start
To tell him he was but a lamb...
She didn't have the heart.

Berber was a carefree lamb
Who never wore a frown.
A smile was always on his face,
And nothing got him down.

'Twas a thrill to hear him speak...
He had a lovely Baaa.
Whenever people heard him, they
Would always "ooh" and "ahhh."

Berber ran and bucked and jumped,
And sometimes you might find
Him running toward you at full speed
To butt you from behind.

He ate his food with pleasure
Whenever he was fed,
But more than anything—he loved...
Strawberries—bright and red.

Berber was a faithful lamb
Who always understood
How beautiful his days could be,
The road of life how good.

Berber left a legacy
Of love right from the start,
For he is Margaret's precious lamb...
His home is in her heart.

MARGARET ANDERSON JOHNSON is pictured here with another one of her pet lambs. Aside from being an author, she has been a Sunday school teacher for fifty years, involved in training Cutting horses, and is currently a potential sheep farmer. Her book is the story of her first lamb, Berber, whom she loved very much.

Margaret grew up in Knoxville, Tennessee, and lives on WaterOak Plantation in Tallahassee, Florida next to Millstone Plantation, an historically preserved sheep farm. Her husband Tom C. Johnson, is a retired business executive and World War II D-Day veteran of Omaha Beach. They have three children and five grandchildren.

During her seventy two years, Margaret has nurtured all types of animals through uncertain, shaky, and wobbly babyhoods. She has raised horses, dogs, cats, ducks, squirrels, and of course, little wooly lambs...especially one lamb in particular, Berber. His true story was begging to be told...

For addtional copies of

Berber
A Lamb's Tale

Order from:
WaterOak Publishing
6056 Thomasville Road
Tallahassee, FL 32312

$15.95 each, plus $3.50 shipping & handling first copy. ($1.50 each additional.)
Sales tax for Florida orders.